The
Kingdom

Benjamin T. Collier

THE KINGDOM

ISBN: 978-1-77069-219-0

Printed in Canada.

Word Alive Press
131 Cordite Road, Winnipeg, MB R3W 1S1
www.wordalivepress.ca

MIX
Paper from
responsible sources
FSC® C016245

Library and Archives Canada Cataloguing in Publication

Collier, Benjamin T., 1983-
    The kingdom / Benjamin T. Collier.

ISBN 978-1-77069-219-0

    I. Title.

PS8605.O457K56 2010   C813'.6   C2010-907890-X

ACKNOWLEDGEMENTS

First off – thank you to my family and friends for their ongoing encouragement over the years; Ray Wiseman (and team) for seeing the writer that I could be and guiding me on that path; The Word Guild, not only for the help you guys have given me as a writer but also for the fellowship; my mum and dad for their ongoing support; big sisters Anna and Karen for encouraging me in my work. My friends, to all of whom I'm very thankful, are now too many to mention on one page, but I will mention Shanks because he's had dibs for eighteen years now. I also want to thank the Alpha team, who I've been glad to have in my life for the past four years – you guys rock! Thank you to everyone at Word Alive Press who saw the potential in this story and who helped to give me the opportunity to share it. A big thank you to everyone who has prayed for me on this journey.

Thank You God for all the different, unique ways You tell me that You love me. Thank You that I am forgiven, and for not giving up on me. Thank You for this passion, and for the strength to get this far.

The kingdom of heaven suffers violence,
And violent men take it by force.

Matthew 11:12

CHAPTER ONE

The cobblestone streets were packed with horses and wagons, and men of every age, race, and stature. Heroes and warriors, warlords and princes all forced their way into the main square before the steps leading up to the castle—each man followed closely by his own personal entourage and horses pulling in carts filled with their most treasured possessions. The sun rose into a clear blue sky without a cloud in sight, shedding unfiltered light on everything and everyone in the square.

The castle of the kingdom of Allandor stood tall and mighty on the slopes rising over the city. It was a vast structure built of the brightest stone, shining gold and silver and styled in the most celestial cloud and starburst patterns by artisans whose legendary craft had long since left this world. Embedded in the center, but more difficult to glimpse through the encircling watchtowers, was the inner palace, a gem in the center of lesser gems as the eye of a flower surrounded by its pedals, shining with the light of every precious jewel.

Waterfalls decorated each of the towering structures. Streams of water burst forth from fountains, poured down the sides of the buildings into the moat, and traveled to the inner pumping system where they began their journey anew. The waterfalls lent a cleansing feel to the beauty of the castle—a perpetual purity—and the illusion that the towers were ever ascending.

Surrounding the castle was a thick black wall that wound all the way around the top of the slope. Its only gate stood at the front, facing the city. Every seventh step up toward the castle gates bore these engravings, inscripted into the stone long ago: ON THESE STEPS YE SHALL BE WEIGHED.

Lord Lucas sat uncomfortably on a very comfortable throne, his eyes shifting warily across the crowd. The throne, carried out and placed at the head of the steps while surrounded by armed guards, was the largest throne in the known world—the throne of Allandor. Here he had ruled as Steward for a full decade, elected by the people when the king sailed off on an expedition to seek land in the West. A shadeless sky piled onto the heat he already felt from his thick robes and the chainmail he wore underneath. The sweat made his long dark hair cling to his skin like black veins. Even the cloth tent his servants held over him couldn't hide him from the punishing sun; nothing could hide from those piercing rays.

He dreaded days like this one, necessary as they were. He had seen it all before. Every weekend for the past few months had brought the same parties. Not the same people, but they might as well have been. Endless precessions of *Prince* this and *Lord* that and *Legendary Hero* whatever followed by displays of gold and weapons and the head of their latest kill. He had never been excited about these visits, but it was not for him that these presentations were brought.

A deafening cheer rose from the great throng as Princess Nevaeh was carried out seated on her own throne, which required far fewer servants to lift than the true throne of Allandor. Her gaze did not lift from the ground when the flood of people welcomed her, and her composure was as frozen as a statue despite the wobbling of her seat. The servants let her throne down beside Lucas and immediately they began waving palm branches for her, creating a soothing breeze. She shuffled only once, making herself as comfortable as she could manage for the long, long hours ahead.

It was for her that all these men had come. She was young, attractive, and heir to the largest throne in the known world. By Allandor custom, she could not take the throne until she married, and the year for that was mere weeks away. Men had come from all corners of the world to seize this rare opportunity.

The presentations began immediately. The ascending outbursts over who should go first had of course been dealt with long before the lady came out, lest she witness anything uncouth. The first lord ascended the steps wearing what was very likely his most elaborate and expensive robe, and certainly his most arrogant smile.

"Lord Alaric Gualterio of Estelasia!" the announcer proclaimed. "General of the Chimera Legions and Captain of the *Silver Mermaid*."

Well-built and exotic servants carried up carts loaded with gold and jewels while a bard recited poems dedicated to his highness' exploits.

Boroccas the Mountain-Strong stepped up afterward carrying several dragon heads and piling them onto the ground before reciting his own exploits, his eyes shining with great pride.

On and on it went throughout the day, some even proudly displaying what they had stolen from others, hoping their roguish charm would endear themselves to the princess. When evening finally fell, the princes brought out their fire-dancers.

Lucas observed the princess periodically throughout the day. This weekend had been no more successful than all those before. She could barely keep her eyes open! During Onimon Giacomo's tale of his duel with a Cyclops, she actually yawned, not even making the slightest effort to stifle it. Had she no sense of propriety? Lucas cared little for the parades, true, but the princess at least should have shown some appreciation for all these attempts at wooing her.

When she started bobbing her head with her eyes closed, the royal announcer informed the crowd that that would be all. Offended murmurs rose from the barely thinning crowd still jumbled in the square, but when the servants came to carry the princess away on her throne the crowd finally dispersed. By the time the two dozen servants came to carry Lucas away on his throne, he was not at all in an agreeable mood.

THE THRONE ROOM WAS always dimly lit at this time of night. Torches on massive pillars lit the expansive room. One could barely see the end of the high ceiling that seemed to stretch into infinity.

The servants, catching the moods of their lord and lady, had offered to call in the jesters. When Lucas declined with a lazy wave of his hand, everyone hurried to their own tasks in any other room but this one and let Lucas and the princess sit alone on their thrones.

A long time they sat in silence. Lucas sat up straight and lordly despite his discomfort, but the lady slouched sideways, resting her head on her fist. Her teachers had not been nearly strict enough.

"That went as well as could be expected," Lucas said in his cheery tone. "Did anyone catch your eye today?"

The princess was silent.

After a moment, he tried again. "Did you fancy anyone from a previous week? Do you remember his name?"

She ignored him completely.

The cheer left his voice. "Princess, your coronation day is fast approaching. You must choose a suitor by then and, although your womanly mind has raised certain expectations, you have only what is available to choose from." He leaned toward her and looked to her with warm, fatherly eyes which she continued to ignore. "You need to choose a wise and noble husband who will be able to take care of you."

"I don't need to do anything," she retorted plainly. "My father is returning. He will rule the kingdom. I've no need to choose a king."

She said it all without looking at him once. Lucas fell back in his chair wearily, stifled the angry words he was going to say and, straightening himself again, raised the next question.

"Princess, do you know where your father is?"

"He is in the land beyond the sea. Everyone knows that."

"Yes, that is what people have been saying since you were a child—that he has 'gone to the land beyond the sea.' I would have thought by now that you would have grown out of that naivety." He glanced at her, but saw no response. "It is a metaphorical term, my Lady— there is no land beyond the sea. Your father is dead."

At that, she turned to him with harsh, accusing eyes and said, "You're a liar!" He shook his head sympathetically. "You have no proof! You have no body to bury!"

"Eyewitnesses who watched him sail west reported that a storm hit the ship. He should have known better than to sail under a red sunrise. The waves were large enough to swallow the ship whole, and that is just what they did. Nothing has been seen of it since."

"I don't believe you! My father had the gift of prophecy. He knew his voyage would be successful and that he would return."

"I won't debate with you whether he was a prophet or not—that does not matter. What matters is that you consider what is best for the kingdom now. Choose a noble suitor, one who is familiar with the affairs of a kingdom, and the people will adore you no longer as simply the Princess but as their Queen. It was what your father wanted."

The princess jumped out of her chair and stood facing him. Despite his height even sitting down, she seemed to tower over him as she aimed a finger directly between his eyes.

"This much is certain—if there was even the faintest doubt in my father's mind that he may not return, he would never have allowed the kingdom to fall into your crooked hands! And I'll thank you kindly not to speak of my father in the past tense. He lives! And the throne will be pulled out from under you on his return!"

With that, she turned her back to him and stormed away. Lucas could hear her footsteps echo thunderously through the room until she finally slammed a door behind her. At once, he exhaled all his pent-up fury and jumped off the throne to pace through the room, hands on his sweat-drenched head.

"You may be familiar with the affairs of the kingdom," said a familiar voice, "but for you, my Lord, the heart is still foreign territory."

Lucas turned and saw Theodius standing among the pillars, a bearded man not ten years older than himself, wrapped in a cloak elegant enough to suit the Steward's adviser.

"How much of that did you hear?"

"Nothing you wouldn't have told me yourself."

Lucas shook his head and spread his arms out in submission. "She is a hard woman. I can only get through to her by logic."

"She is too young to understand the needs of her kingdom. If you wish to win her heart, you must hone your wooing skills, which are in much need of oiling. Discontinue the suitor presentations and focus on the two of you."

Lucas waved that idea aside. "She hates me with the greatest hatred I have ever seen in a woman's eyes. I cannot win her heart that way or any other way. But I know how much she despises these suitors, and the more she comes to realize that every other lord is the same the more she will be to choose the one who has already held the throne for ten years. The presentations will continue."

"But remember, my Lord, that she need not necessarily choose anyone. The laws say she must choose a suitor by her eighteenth birthday to ascend to the throne, but if she does not then she would be abdicating—and to whom will the throne go in such a case?"

"It may very well go to the next of kin, should she wish to take it—her Aunt Mary, who is already betrothed!"

"An accident can easily befall her."

"I will not resort to that. Not yet. Not unless every other plan falls through. The less blood I have on my hands, the better."

"The blood will not be on your hands, my Lord."

Lucas fell silent and gave him an appreciative glance. It was because of Theodius that Lucas had become Steward. In the absence of the king, Allandor was instructed to follow the ancient laws, looking to a committee of appointed landlords rather than a single head over the whole kingdom. Theodius had persuaded the people to vote for new leadership instead, and they had elected Lucas as Steward.

Lucas and Theodius were both willing to employ any tactics necessary to see the kingdom in the right hands. Lucas wanted so much to be done with this current strategy, yet his continuing rule as Steward would never be as indisputable as his rule as King.

"The presentations will continue."

THE PRINCESS MARCHED through the halls as swiftly as her dress would allow. Any servants who saw her observed the look in her eyes and hugged the walls. She fiddled with the necklace through her dress, the one her father had given her just before his expedition. A "matrimonial necklace," he had called it. He always told her how wise and intelligent she was, and that the time would come when she would give the necklace to a man of her choosing, and that he would be instantly bound to her, and she to him. He trusted that she would make the right decision, yet so far, after all these presentations, she had found no one.

One man with stubble and a shaved head greeted her with, "How is my Lady this evening?"

"Fine, Lord Daxion," she said without thinking and walked right past, bounding up a flight of stairs.

Daxion turned around and said gently, "Does my Lady wish to know how I am?"

Nevaeh stopped halfway up, embarrassed. She turned around and curtsied. "I beg your pardon, Lord Captain. How are you?"

Finally she looked him in the eyes. He had beautiful, piercing, bright blue eyes that went well with his striking face. "I am well, Princess…though I am a little worried about you."

"It has been a very long day," she said with a sigh and a tired smile.

"Is there anything I can do to serve my Lady?"

He was looking at her with that fond stare again—a look both strong and vulnerable that said he truly would do anything if she only asked. She took a few steps back down and returned his glare.

"Do you believe my father is a prophet?"

He blinked, and instantly his face changed to that well-known face he wore during political campaigns. "There is no one in all the kingdom who would question your father, my Lady."

"I am not asking you what the Lord Captain would declare to the public…" She stepped all the way down until they spoke eye-to-eye. "I am asking you, Daxion, to tell me, Nevaeh, what… you… believe."

He looked her in the eyes for a moment longer before answering, "My beliefs, Princess, have never held sway over my service to Lord Lucas—to the kingdom."

She sighed in disappointment and gave him a patronizing smile. "I expected no less," she said before heading back up the stairs.

"If I may be so bold, my Lady…" She stopped and turned to face him once more, her skirt flowing as she pivoted. "I see that these presentations have taken a heavy toll on you. I had hoped for some time now that you would look upon me with such favour that you might cancel these presentations."

She chuckled. "Why suffer these shows every weekend when I could be married to one? That is not what I desire. Goodnight, Lord Daxion."

She continued up the stairs and onto the next floor when she heard a barely audible, "Goodnight… Princess Nevaeh."

NEVAEH SAT IN her bed in the Princess' chambers, her back resting against pillows freshly fluffed by Gilda, the plump lady-in-waiting who was just now setting a tray of warm tea by the bed. The herbal aroma warmed her almost as much as the thick blankets. Nevaeh held in her hand a large storybook with illustrations like the kind her father had read to her as a child. Fairy tales, everyone said, though her father always quoted the characters' lines as if from memory.

"Do you think it foolish?" asked Nevaeh.

"Do I think what foolish, my Lady?" responded Gilda as she tucked the bed sheets further in.

"Waiting for someone sensible."

"Oh, not at all, dear. I think you're well in your right mind. It's the rest of the world that's foolish."

"It's just… hour after hour, week after week they're all the same. They're all so fake."

She remembered her first kiss… if one could call it that. When she was ten, one of the local princes had approached her during a land-wide celebration, said a few well-rehearsed regal words, and pecked her on the lips. It had all been a show; she had gotten nothing out of it besides a small sense of violation. He strutted away without even looking for a reaction in her eyes and likely bragged to all the other princes later that night about how she had thrown herself upon him like a farm girl. Every lord she had seen in these weekend presentations had been like that little boy, grown bigger but not grown up. Were all real princes like that?

She brought herself back to the present and observed in her book a picture of a valiant knight climbing a dark, treacherous, monster-infested tower to rescue the beautiful maiden trapped inside. The next page would show the wedding reception at their dream palace. She wondered how many girls dreamed the kind of dreams she did.

A FULL MOON hung high over the land, veiled by thick clouds that cut off the light as they glided silently across its luminous face. Torches alone were barely enough to light the ways of the palace guards as they made their rounds through the inner courts and across the stone bridges that connected the various watchtowers hemmed in by the black wall. The palace stood in the center of the grounds, glimmering ghostly pale in the night.

Pairs of black wings circled around a high tower in clusters, squawking, casting their shapes on the ground far below in shadows darker than the rest of the night. A single, far larger shadow passed across the grounds on a straight path, and then the glass window of the high tower shattered.

"I SUGGEST WE increase the tax on the South crossing," said Theodius as he observed a book in his hands while standing amongst a clutter of papers and books in the Steward's study.

"We have many kings coming in from the South," Lucas said from his desk, searching through papers, "I wouldn't want to insult them. I'll need their support if we…" A faint and unfamiliar ringing sound caught the attention of both men. "What is that?"

Theodius lowered the book in his hand and listened intently. "Is that the alarm bell?"

Suddenly the ring resounded into a harsh clang and fell silent.

"Yes," Lucas thought aloud. "I think that was the alarm bell."

A guard barged into the room without knocking, fear paining his face.

"My Lords, come with me, I pray to safety—there is an intruder!"

Inside the south tower, guards charged through corridors, up and down staircases, toward the sound of smashing stone and screaming men, to meet in the hall a large, black shape lifting men off the ground and tossing them into the walls. Those with time to shout pleaded for aid to anyone in earshot and reinforcements of every kind poured into the hall. A man around the corner managed to nock an arrow just before he was batted aside by large talons.

Surrounded by dozens of guards, Lucas hurried across a stone bridge as he was led to the palace by the captain of the guards, Lord Daxion. He was closed in lest any arrow-fire should reach him as the captain led him to the palace. Every torch on the grounds had been lit and he could see the many towers aglow, most of all the palace whose walls reflected the frenzied flames.

"We have safe rooms in the palace for such an emergency, Sire," said Daxion, trying to sound unshaken. "Every soldier on the grounds is hastening to the south tower. The intruder is closed off. He will not be able to—"

Shattering glass called attention to the south tower and Lucas vaguely saw a black, winged creature crash through more stained-glass windows into the east tower.

Only then did Lucas realize he had been forced to the floor by several guards who had dropped flat on their bellies. The guards all rose again as Daxion erected himself.

"All guards to the east tower!" he shouted to the guards below. The order was echoed across the grounds. Daxion grabbed Lucas' arm himself and forced him to rush harder toward the safety of the palace. They had only taken a few swift strides before another window of the east tower shattered and the black creature flew toward the palace.

Daxion paused. Then, with a grave face, he gestured to four of his men, saying, "Take the Lord Steward into the barracks. There may be some spare rooms there. The rest of you, come with me."

"The palace," Lucas noted as the four men turned

him around to run the other way. "Nevaeh is in there."

Then he heard Daxion shout as he ran full-stride across the bridge, "Release Venommane!"

THE ORDER WAS repeated into the dark, hidden chambers of the palace. Two guards whose sole purpose was to wait for that call pulled individual levers on either side of a wall of metal bars, causing it to rise into the ceiling. Out pounced a lion ten times the size of any normal lion, with a scorpion's tail and a wild-faced man in crude battle-armour sitting on its back with a spiked whip. The beast roared as if it had just topped a mountain, causing the low ceiling to quake.

A light tap from the whip made the creature charge out of the chamber and leap up the spiralling stairs into the hall, crushing any man in its path until it rounded one corner, toppled over, and rolled into the wall with an arrow deep in its eye. Thrown off, the rider smacked into a wall and fell to the floor beside his deceased pet, unable to move.

A man completely covered in dark clothes and scarves of various shades approached him from a large, winged creature and held an axe blade to the rider's face.

"You don't look a man who's loyal to the point of torture and death," said the dark man. "Where is Princess Nevaeh?"

Gilda clenched Nevaeh's hand so tight that it hurt as she forced her into a secret room.

"You'll be safe in here, my Lady."

"But there's no light!"

Gilda ignored her protest. "Now don't come out for anything—not for anyone." She hurried out to close the door behind her.

"What are you going to do?" Nevaeh pleaded. When the door was shut and sealed, darkness enveloped her. "What are you going to do!" She heard no answer. In fact, she could hear nothing. Darkness and silence. She felt for a surface resembling a chair and, finding nothing, resorted to sitting on the stone floor. She felt so stifled in that place after just a short time that it was a shock to her when she heard a vague thudding vibrating through the floor.

THE GUARDS INSIDE the Princess' inner chambers had barricaded the doors with everything to be found— including the bed, tables, chairs, and drawers—and now they held their own bodies against it as the living battering ram continued to beat upon it, the doors splintering and bending into the chamber more and more with each thrust. The bloodthirsty shriek from the other side was that of a conquering predator about to feast.

THE DOOR INTO the palace swung open with great force, allowing Daxion and his men into a large room where lay the body of the great lion. A few pale-faced guards standing idly about the room gave their captain a relieved look as he entered.

"We're safe for now, Captain," said one. "The creature has moved to the higher levels."

"And the Princess?" demanded Daxion.

Every guard looked away or to the floor, shuffling his feet. Daxion drew his sword and ran up the nearest stairway with all his might.

"Captain!" shouted one guard. "It's too dangerous!"

"Then don't follow me!" Daxion shouted back as he disappeared upstairs.

THE DOORS TO the Princess' inner chambers burst open with men and splintered wood flying everywhere. The hideous face of the serpent-necked creature thrust itself into the room, wide-eyed with a triumphant shriek, and the dark man leaped off its back brandishing his axe.

THE THUDDING HAD stopped. Nevaeh tried to hold her breath so she could hear what else was going on, but she could not make anything out from the jumble of barely audible noises. The only thing she heard clearly was some kind of inhuman shrieking.

The Princess' inner chamber had become a torn and battered mess cluttered with fallen men. The black beast stood in the doorway with its head high, sniffed the air in the room, snorted, and clicked its forked tongue.

The dark man observed that a single bookshelf had not been touched in the scramble to barricade the door, and leisurely walked over to find out why.

A plump woman wielding a kitchen knife pounced out from a nearby curtain and the dark man grabbed her by the wrists.

"So much as touch her and I'll knife you like a pig, you fiend!" the woman shouted.

His forehead met her face and she fell unconscious. He tossed her aside and began fingering the bookshelf for hidden switches. The black creature shook itself off from its head all the way down to its tail, making the jewellery in its pointed ears and tailfins jingle.

The door creaked open and light poured into the room, blocking Nevaeh's vision of who had come to her rescue. An unfamiliar and unfriendly voice greeted her.

"I've found you."

She screamed and tried to run, but it did no good. He grabbed her, bound her hands behind her with a rough cloth, and carried her out on his shoulders, kicking and screaming. She screamed even louder when she saw the giant, black beast standing in the doorway, looking down on her like a crow on a helpless rodent.

The creature let its back down so the man could lift her onto it, lying on her belly. The man climbed on, grabbed onto a leather strap attached to the creature's back, and made a strange noise. The beast raced toward the balcony of the Princess' audience chamber and leaped out the window. Nevaeh screamed again, though by now she was losing her voice. Within an instant, she was looking down on the palace grounds—the same view she had always seen from her balcony she now saw from mid-air with no foundations holding her up. The man turned around to fire arrows at soldiers following them on Gryphon-back. It wasn't long before the few Gryphons fast enough to keep up all plummeted to the city.

The thick clouds retreated to the horizons, revealing the stars and the full, brilliant moon shedding perfect, pale light onto the world. The black, winged creature sped through the night sky, the familiar kingdom below passing by at great speed, giving way to new lands further north—an unfamiliar wilderness of forest and mountains. Princess Nevaeh looked up at the dark-covered man who had abducted her, his faceless mask staring off into the unknown with reckless ambition. At last, she fainted.

CHAPTER TWO

Lucas sat eerily on the throne of Allandor rubbing his forehead thoroughly. Many men stood before him, all wearing guilt-ridden faces. Daxion stood among them, just as perplexed by the previous night as everyone else, and just as afraid.

"How did this happen?" Lucas asked. His eyes, steady on the floor, gave no indication of whom he was asking.

Daxion spoke first. "It is my fault, Lord, forgive me. I did not expect it to become an aerial pursuit—until it was too late. Our men have not been trained for this scenario."

Lucas lifted his head and locked his shadowy eyes on the captain. "Why not?"

"Proper training procedures have never been a priority in the kingdom, my Lord." Daxion's eyes involuntarily flashed in Theodius' direction.

Theodius spoke up. "Just this past decade, we became the first kingdom to successfully tame Gryphons and Pegasus for military service, despite the training difficulties. No one could have predicted the enemy would acquire the aid of Dragons."

"We do not know it was a Dragon," Daxion corrected.

"What else can out-fly Gryphons?"

"If you would spend more time observing the reality of the dangers around this kingdom, you might know!"

"Enough!" Lucas bellowed. "I don't care! The Princess is gone! How do we get her back?" He slammed his fist on the armrest. The room fell silent.

"We know they were heading north," answered Daxion. "But with no ground trail, it will be difficult to track. I will speak to the local hunters and see if there are any aerial beasts that can pick up the scent. If that fails, we will have to wait for the kidnapper to reveal his plans, and then move once we know his intentions."

NEVAEH WOKE TO the feel of hot air blowing on her face. Opening her eyes, she saw the Thing's face almost touching hers. She let out a coarse wail, scrambling to get away, but her hands were bound to a tree behind her. All she could do was kick her legs and scream. A hand covered her mouth and she looked into the masked face of her kidnapper, kneeling down to her, motioning with his other hand for her to be silent.

"You're scaring the food away," he told her. Then he took his hand off her mouth and started rummaging through a cluster of stones on the ground, picked some up, and threw them away.

She was in an open area, a clearing in the middle of a forest of tall trees. Judging by the light, it was late morning. The ground was packed dirt and littered with rocks and pebbles, almost like a beach. She could see a few boulders as well, and logs encircling a pile of chopped wood and sticks in the center. She could hear a brook nearby, but no wildlife. What animals would dare draw attention to themselves with a Dragon in their midst? The Thing still had its nose to her, its putrid breath snorting on her. She squealed.

"Call off your Dragon! I don't like the way he's looking at me!"

"*She* is a Wyvern," the man said as he honed his knife with a carefully selected stone.

"Is she going to eat me?"

Standing over her, the man lightly kicked her bare legs and said, "These flimsy things? What would be the point?" She looked up at him in horror. She couldn't tell if his voice was sympathetic or threatening. He stared at her with unseen eyes as if awaiting a certain response. Then, giving up, he walked away and said, "She won't eat you unless I cook you first. She's addicted to my cooking—won't eat anything raw." He walked over to a log on which several things had been spread out, but she paid them little attention.

"She's sniffing me!"

"She probably likes the way you smell—which amazes me. When you Royals aren't bathing in tubs of perfume, you stink as bad as everyone else." He was now taking a flask of ointment out of a pocket in her robe, which was when she realized she was in nothing but a short nightgown.

"You derobed me!" she shouted. "You pig! What else did you do while I was in a susceptible state?"

He walked over to her with knife in hand. She instinctively drew herself to the tree as tight as she could.

"A princess is worth a lot of money," he said, leaning over her. "A virgin princess is worth more. Now try to be quiet."

He grabbed her hair and she felt him yank on it as if trying to pull it off. Suddenly she was loose and he walked back to the log carrying a lock of hair.

"What are you going to do with me?"

He didn't answer but grabbed the flask and poured an absurd amount of it onto the lock of hair.

"Hey! That ointment is expensive!"

"I'm sure you'll agree that your freedom is worth more."

Closing the flask, he wrapped the hair in a small roll of paper and sealed it with string.

"Who do you think you are, attacking the palace, breaking into my chambers, bringing me out here, and spilling my ointments!?"

He faced her instantly, stepped toward her with

the roll of paper in his hand and with the other hand pulled off the mask that hid him.

He was a man, in his mid-twenties maybe, with white skin, scruffy light-brown hair, and brown eyes. His hair looked like it hadn't been combed in days and the sweat positioned it in odd ways. His face was an unbalanced blend of stubble, clean-shaven and patches of full beard accompanied by scars. When he opened his chapped lips, he revealed uneven teeth. Without pride or shame, he said, "I'm Roy."

After that, he just looked at her, as if daring her to give a better response. She straightened herself as best as she could while lying on the dirt and said, "Well, I'm Princess Nevaeh! Heir to the throne of Allandor! I am your future Queen, and I command you to return my robe to me!"

Before she knew it, her robe was blocking her vision, just thrown onto her face. She tried to pull it off and was aptly reminded that her hands were still bound to the tree. Kicking with all her might, she caught the robe on her foot and pulled it from her face. The Wyvern was still sniffing her, so she threw the robe at it. The beast finally walked away and followed its master into the forest.

It was supposed to be a discussion of how the search was going and what needed to be done next, but instead the meeting in the Steward's study turned into a shouting match between Daxion and Theodius, with

Lucas struggling just to get a few words in.

With them was Bruce, the bald, burly man Daxion had hired to lead the search for the princess. "An old comrade," Daxion had said. He looked like a ruffian to Lucas, especially with that scar just under his eye, but if he could help get the princess back, Lucas would make him a Lord.

"Listen to me, Theodius!" Daxion insisted. "There is no scent. The Pegasus cannot pick up the trail in the air. We have to focus our search on the ground!"

"The trail is there," Theodius argued "You just need better hounds. A Pegasus couldn't smell its own refuse if it walked backward!"

"Is it possible she's still in the area?" Lucas spoke up. "We shouldn't assume she was taken northward with the black beast. That may have been a misdirection."

"There is no scent in the area, my Lord," Daxion reminded him.

"There is no scent outside the area, either!"

A guard entered the room with a small scroll. "A message for my Lord the Steward."

"Not now!" Lucas roared at the guard before pointing his finger back at Daxion. "You said yourself your hounds have not picked up anything outside the Princess' room. That means she could be anywhere!"

Theodius took the scroll from the guard's hand and unrolled it while Daxion countered. "Our hounds know the Lady's perfume very well. If she were any-where in the city, she would have been found by now."

"If you wish to see Princess Nevaeh alive, you will follow my instructions." All heads turned to Theodius as he read aloud from the scroll. "You have two days to—"

Lucas snatched the scroll from his hands and read it silently.

Daxion picked up a lock of hair that fell from it and lifted it to his nose. "This is the Lady's perfume."

Once Lucas finished reading the scroll, he handed it to Daxion. "Do as he says." Daxion and Bruce read it together as Lucas addressed the guard. "Who delivered this message?"

"A carrier hawk, my Lord. It is still here."

"Keep it here until I say so. Daxion, come with me."

Lucas quickly led Daxion out of the room and through the halls toward a more private study. The surly Bruce followed without permission, but Lucas wasted no time lecturing him.

"Would we be able to follow the hawk back to its master?" Daxion asked as they paced on.

"We can certainly try," Bruce answered with a foreign accent. "But if this man knows what he's doing, he'll 'ave trained it not to return until it knows it's not being followed."

Lucas ignored the conversation behind him and hurried on, turning down one last corner and bursting through a dark door. Once in his private study, he went straight to his desk, grabbed a small piece of paper and a pen, and began writing hurriedly, speaking as he did.

"I'm writing a letter of response to this fiend so no harm will befall the Lady. The instant I hand this to you, see that it reaches the carrier hawk. Once that's done, you will send men throughout the city, throughout the palace, throughout the land as far east as time permits, to be certain our kidnapper is pleased with our compliance. We must see the Princess back at all costs." He crumpled up that paper furiously, tossed it, and began writing on another.

Daxion looked back over the words in the little scroll as if it were a joke. "Surely, my Lord, we won't simply give in to these demands."

"What options have we?" he burst out. He went back to writing and then, noticing the silence, looked back to Daxion and Bruce and observed the sly, experienced, assertive grin they both wore. With a calmer tone, Lucas asked again, "What options have we?"

It was some time in the afternoon when Nevaeh woke again, her muscles aching horribly. Wrestling with her bonds had done nothing but wear out what little energy she had. When the sound of footsteps drew nearer, she realized what had woken her up. Roy came out of the forest brandishing his knife, his face neutral as before with just the faintest frown. He walked straight toward her.

Nevaeh sat up as high as she could with her hands still touching the ground. Roy knelt down expressionless and began cutting the rope with his knife.

"You're releasing me?" she exclaimed with surprise.

"That depends on your definition of release."

She observed his face for any sign of his intentions but found nothing. "But you *are* untying me?"

"We have a lot of walking to do. I'd rather not carry you everywhere. And you're obviously not a threat. So yes, I'm untying you."

He threw her cut bonds aside, stood up, and walked away, turning his back to her.

"I'll run," she warned.

He stopped and looked at her with a raised eyebrow. "Go ahead. If you think you can find your way back... hunt food, build a fire... do you know what to do if you're surrounded by wolves?"

"Okay, I see your point," she said with her head low. "Where are we going?"

"Come and see."

He walked deeper into the forest and, after some hesitation, Nevaeh rose to follow him.

THEY HADN'T GONE far before Roy led her to a heavily-shaded forest area where the sunlight only broke through in flittering patches of light that danced in the soft breeze. Scattered twigs snapped softly under her bare feet. The ground was cold and dirty, and occasional patches of grass tickled her feet without warning. She didn't know what she was stepping on half the time.

From a distance, she saw the Wyvern carry massive lumps of something indiscernible on its back and in its teeth. The lump in its mouth opened and colours spilled out of it onto a larger pile of colours on the ground.

Nevaeh observed the colours on the ground. They were clothes—women's clothes, and certainly more colourful than any she had ever worn. Half of them were just various undergarments and the outer clothing wasn't more decent by much. Some of them were even jewel-encrusted.

"The nights are cold in the woods," he told her as he opened another bag. "I suggest you pick something warm, and a blanket to go with it."

"Whose are these?"

"They're mine," Roy answered.

Nevaeh looked to a busty, scarlet brassier on the ground and gave him a more questioning glare.

"They're articles I've acquired over the years." He gave her an intentionally too-innocent look. "I loan them out to women I become familiar with." She meant to give him an accusing glare, but it came out fearful. "There are no strings attached," he assured her. "I don't want to decrease your value, remember?"

"What is it you plan to do with me?" she demanded.

"My goal, Princess, is to get rid of you as soon as possible. If all goes well, you'll be back in your palace in a short time, bathing in gold and drinking perfume.

But who knows how long that will be, so in the meantime I suggest you make yourself as comfortable as you can in the real world." He opened the last bag.

Nevaeh suppressed her anger. If she became aggressive, she may be bound again.

"Where can I change?"

He gave her an analyzing glare, eyebrow raised, then looked around the forest and said, "Pick a tree." Then he walked off, with the Wyvern following close behind.

"I can trust you not to take advantage of me?"

He chortled and continued walking.

FINDING THREE TREES close together, Nevaeh used long scarves to make an encircling clothesline and set up the blankets to hide herself as she changed. Roy had also provided a stand-up mirror, which she rested against one of the trees. The Wyvern came back a couple of times to sniff at her from above and left when Nevaeh threw brassieres at it.

As she got out of her nightgown, she realized that she was still wearing her necklace. Her kidnapper hadn't noticed it. If she wished to keep it, she would have to find some clothes with a place to hide it, which looked like it would be a challenge.

There was very little she wanted her captor to see her in, much less whoever rescued her. There were no tops with high necklines and nearly every skirt stopped above her knees. The only skirts that reached her ankles had gaping slits along the side. She decided to wear one of those together with the thickest stockings she could find.

Most of the corsets she wouldn't even touch. The shapes and designs put a lot of emphasis where she didn't want it. She tried on a plain one, and when she saw herself in the mirror… *Oh…* She looked at herself again. Then sideways. She had never worn anything that did that. As a matter of fact, they didn't make anything like that for the Royal Family of Allandor. It might not hurt to wear this, but she would need an extra-decent top to go with it.

The tops she quickly sorted into a pile of *Maybe* and a much larger pile of *Never*. She found a strange top that covered the back and the arms—she could hide the necklace in a sleeve—but it left much of the front uncovered. Finding nothing better, she settled on that and wrapped a scarf around her neck, stretching it to cover as much of her skin as it could.

She selected a pair of sandals and a warm blanket with leopard spots and stepped out of her mini-dressing room.

Roy was sitting outside on a rock. When he saw her, he had a hint of disappointment in his eyes.

"That's… different," he said patronizingly.

Did he actually expect her to dress like his woman-friends? "There wasn't much to choose from," she said.

He blinked. "Alright, let's head back." He got up and started walking back toward the open forest.

Nevaeh followed at a distance.

When they returned to what Nevaeh recognized as the campsite, she asked, "Where's your pet?"

"Catching the rest of our dinner. I caught a few snacks earlier, but not enough for the three of us."

A hawk cry rang through the air. Roy lifted his head and raised an arm. To Nevaeh's surprise, the hawk swooped down out of nowhere right onto Roy's arm, flapping its wings as it landed before settling them behind its back. Nevaeh remained at a distance while Roy stroked its head, took a small piece of paper attached to the hawk's leg, unrolled it and read it thoroughly.

"What is it?" Nevaeh asked.

Roy glanced at her, then grinned.

"Good news."

He put the paper in his pocket, kissed the hawk on the side of its head, and whispered a strange noise into its ear. The hawk flew off into the air and disappeared behind the trees. Just as it did, the Wyvern swooped into the campsite with a whole deer in its mouth, spat it onto the ground, and took off again. Nevaeh froze at the sight of it.

"Ah," said Roy. "Time to start the fire."

WHEN THE NIGHT closed in, enveloping the forest, the only light for miles was the campfire. Roy sat on a log in front of the fire eating roasted deer leg. A few small flasks of seasoning rested in a bag at his side. In the thick darkness of the woods, the Wyvern feasted on its own, much larger portion of the deer with many other corpses yet to devour, all professionally cooked. Its earrings jingled as it gnawed its dinner in the surrounding darkness.

Nevaeh had been reluctant to join the feasting up until now. She hated being close to Roy, but she hated even more being in the darkness of the woods. She stepped closer to the fire with the leopard blanket wrapped around her. Roy grabbed a chunk of meat and held it out to her. She looked at it, a little disturbed.

"What is it?"

"Rabbit," he said between chewing. She felt a little more disturbed. Roy blinked to hide the fact that his eyes were rolling. "It died quickly. And if I hadn't caught it, a wolf would have, and they aren't so merciful."

She took it from his hand as if casually deciding that she may as well. She bit into it and swallowed quickly before her stomach rumbled again. It wasn't bad, though it had a stronger flavour than what she was used to. She sat down on the log opposite Roy while she ate and tried to stifle her choking when she swallowed too fast. Roy grabbed a poking stick and began shifting the logs in the fire while his other hand held the rest of his meal.

For the first time, she almost felt like she was back at the palace, sitting toasty in front of a roaring fire, cocooned in a blanket. She observed Roy through the fire, his own eyes intent on the flames and the logs he moved. She studied his features, the way he dressed, his apparent experience with campfires, and made a decision.

"You're a Northlander," she announced.

Roy looked up. "Excuse me?"

"All those scarves you wear—I recognize their styling. They're from the Northlands."

He gave her a questioning glare. "If I were from the Northlands, why would I be wearing so many scarves this far south?" Her stare fell to the ground. "I did a lot of raiding up north. I visited a lot of nobles' houses and kept these as souvenirs."

"Oh." The sound of a cracking bone drew her attention back to the darkness where the Wyvern feasted. "Your pet doesn't eat with you?"

"No. The poor thing's afraid of fire. She always sleeps away from camp—at least until the light goes out."

"Does she have a name?"

Roy took a moment to chew an extra large chunk and then answered, "Ruth."

She gave him a lopsided look. "Now why would you name a Wyvern 'Ruth'?"

He took another moment to answer, but this time his mouth was empty and he stared blankly into the fire, jabbing at random kindling. "Because she's the only friend I have." He ceased everything. "And because if anyone ever took her from me…" He looked straight at Nevaeh from across the fire, the flames reflecting off his murderous eyes. It took all Nevaeh's courage not to look away. "…I'd be Ruthless."

She blinked. Roy's face froze in that expression, eyes staring intently. She tried to stare at him the same way, face frozen, but then the faintest curve touched her lips. Roy's lips seemed to curve in response while his eyes stayed frozen. Despite her efforts, Nevaeh smiled and tried to look down before it happened. When she looked up again, Roy was back to prodding the flames, wearing a satisfied grin. She grabbed another piece of meat and scarfed it down in silence.

CHAPTER THREE

The singing of birds woke Nevaeh the next morning. She had not heard birds singing for a while—the Wyvern must be away. Covered in the leopard blanket, she opened her eyes and looked around to see if she could spot the birds.

"Good morning," she heard Roy say. She sat up and turned to see him sitting on the lowest branch of a large tree, slicing an apple with his knife. His face was expressionless, as usual. "How do you feel?"

"I'm alright," she answered, rubbing her back. "How are you?"

He exhaled through his nose and looked up as if struggling to remember before answering, "My neck hurts… I had trouble sleeping. I cut my finger, but it didn't bleed much… and my teeth are starting to ache again." He raised an apple slice to his mouth. "The apples here are good, though."

It wasn't until then that she realized something different about him.

"Your hair's wet."

"I went swimming. There's a pool nearby."

"There's a pool?" That question came out louder than she meant it to. She instantly looked away as if uninterested, wearing the blankest face she could manage. It was one more reminder that she hadn't bathed in more than a day.

"Do you want to go?" he asked.

"Where is it?" she said nonchalantly.

He put the apple down, put his knife away, jumped off the tree, and said, "I'll show you."

NEVAEH FOLLOWED ROY through clearings, shaded forests, over brooks, and uphill until the campsite behind them became shrouded in thick foliage. Rocks were numerous and the grass was scarce, yet crickets thrived here and carried on their mating calls. Nevaeh felt more comfortable here on the high ground where she could see the vibrant blue sky streaked with pure white clouds—the only thing that gave her a sense of freedom.

Freedom... how would she attain it? There were no guidelines for a kidnapping; a palace break-in was "impossible." The only reference she had was from her storybooks, in which the princess often tried to befriend the monster who had taken her.

Roy hacked at several tall plants along the path

and kicked aside large rocks. At least the path was a bit less cluttered for her.

"So, can I ask where you're from?" she ventured. "I know you're not from the north. Are you from the east? The south?"

"Southeast," he answered without turning around. "I grew up in the Minland prairies."

Success! "Minland… That's a good place. They have a good king there."

"He's a Stonewalker. He tried to make the whole kingdom into Stonewalkers." She caught a slight scent of agitation in his voice.

"That's not so bad. Stonewalkers are good people."

"A kingdom of hypocrites is what it became."

She was taken aback. Maybe it wouldn't be so easy to lighten the conversation, but she would try nonetheless. "I suppose that depends on your point of view."

"The title *Stonewalker* carries with it certain expectations—you're always happy, you never complain, you like everybody. If you're not always acting like it's the best day of your life, people look at you like you're foreign, as if being a Stonewalker means you're not allowed to have a bad day."

"You were a Stonewalker?"

"I was raised a Stonewalker."

"I presume you're not one anymore?"

"Weren't you listening?!" The outburst when he turned around shocked her. For the first time, she saw rage in his eyes. "To be a Stonewalker, you have to like everyone! Everything! Everything that happens, good or bad, whether it happens to you or someone you care about! No complaints! No disappointments! No bad days! No, I'm not a Stonewalker! You want to know why? Because I woke up one day and realized I was human!"

He turned his back to her and started walking again, but she stood still a moment.

"Is everything alright?"

"I just told you I have a neck and tooth ache. I can't sleep and I cut myself... and you're asking if everything's alright? What is it with you and stupid questions?"

"I mean, did something happen regarding your plans with me?" She hurried to catch up as his pace quickened. He didn't even bother to clear the path anymore.

"Nothing's changed," he said in a calmer tone.

"Then why are you being so delicate?"

He half-turned, but then kept walking. "Because I'm having a bad morning."

As silence fell on the conversation, Nevaeh searched for the words to break the tension.

"And that's another thing," Roy said. "People are too afraid to be honest with each other. If a woman cleans her friend's windows, but he knows the fluid she uses will just make more work for him, he keeps his mouth shut, because he doesn't want to upset her, even though it gives him twice as much work to do when she leaves. So she keeps coming back to clean his windows, 'cause she thinks she's helping. He just says 'thank you' and does all that work over again. Then one day while she's cleaning, a stranger walks by and explains that she's doing it wrong. So now she feels worse than she would have if the friend had just told her in the first place!"

"Well, it is polite to—"

"People are so terrified of honesty! You must get it even worse, with all your servants afraid of doing even the littlest thing wrong… they gotta make sure the gold in the bathtub's not too hot."

"I don't bathe in gold!"

"We're here."

In her frustration, she hadn't noticed the vague yet escalating sound of rushing water. He had led her to a ridge overlooking a large pool maybe fifteen feet down. There was a waterfall in the distance with vine-covered cliffs on either side. It was surrounded by tall forestry. She began undressing immediately, her frustration almost pushing caution out of her head.

"People think politeness is the answer to everything," he went on. "Politeness doesn't win wars."

"It does a good job of preventing them."

"You can't stop wars. Wars happen whether you're polite or not. But you don't win wars by worrying about everyone's feelings. People need to just be themselves and let everyone else deal with it in their own way. If everyone would just learn to be honest…"

"You know what you are? You're just another arrogant man who thinks he is the answer to everything! You think every problem in the world would instantly dissolve if everybody would just be more like you!"

"Everybody is like me. They just don't want to admit it."

She stood with her arms crossed and glared at him.

"What?" asked Roy.

"You want to turn around?"

It seemed he hadn't realized she was now in nothing but undergarments. He observed her and said, "That may well be the stupidest question you've asked me yet." She glared at him some more. "If you want someone to do something, you don't ask them if they want to do it."

"Turn around!"

"You're not in charge of me." He wore his most satisfied grin yet. Then he toned it down and said, "Look, it's nothing I didn't already get a look at after you passed out."

Her glare trembled. The thought had suddenly made her feel a lot more vulnerable. He still stood with that subtle but obvious grin—watching her, making no effort to be polite or discreet. She turned her back to him anyway as she removed what was left, tried to ignore his presence, and dove off the ridge.

A sudden cold and clean feeling enveloped her as soon as she hit the water. She could see fish frolicking around her at a cautious distance, and closer to the bank she could see water-grass waving in the current like green hair. It felt good to be in any kind of water again. It had been too long since her last bath. It had been even longer since she'd been able to do this in a pool without fear of arousing one of her constant bodyguards. She had no idea why she felt safer here, but she would enjoy it while she could.

ROY WATCHED THE fire as he prodded it with a stick. He had put Nevaeh's clothes on a rock on a sandy spot that sloped to the edge of the pool. Ruth flew in with a dead deer in her mouth, spat it out next to the dead rabbits, and lay down in the sand with her head on the ground, watching Roy at a safe distance.

She always held wonder in her eyes as only an animal could when she watched him cook. She dreaded the fire, yet she desired the food that came from it. That must have been a challenge for her to wrap her head around. He remembered the first time he caught her stealing rabbits from him and running off into the woods. She was no taller than his waist back then, and even after the verbal thrashing he gave her as she scurried off she came back the very next night. That went on for about a week. It wasn't until he captured her and then let her go that she realized she was safe with him. She'd stayed with him ever since.

The sound of splashing water returned his attention to Nevaeh, who was just climbing out of the pool onto the sandy slope. When she saw that he was

43

watching her, she moved to cover herself with her hands, but then deliberately made no effort to and walked toward her clothes with an awkward stride, trying to appear unaware of him. He didn't look away and prodded the fire with little care.

After she had put on her undergarments, he brought his attention back to the fire and said, "Very nice."

He wasn't watching her, but he could feel her puzzled eyes on him.

"I thought you had already seen me."

"I just said that to get you in the pool."

A second of silence went by and then he felt sudden, sharp, intense pain on the back of his head. He dropped his prodding stick right into the fire and yelled just as something else hit his lower back.

"Pig! Brute! Pervert!"

Rocks and names were thrown together in his direction, along with anything else Nevaeh could find. Roy abandoned the fire and ran for cover behind the boulders and trees while his head still spun from the pain. Nevaeh ran up to the fire and threw in Roy's direction a flaming stick that landed right in front of Ruth, making her leap right up and dash into the forest, almost knocking down a tree.

"Boar! Fiend! Beast!"

When Roy saw flaming sticks landing close to the trees, he jumped out of hiding and shouted, "Calm down!"

She stopped throwing things and just stood there with her head in her hands—actually sobbing! Sobbing over what? What was her problem?

"You know what, Princess? Not once have you thanked me for doing you this favour!"

"Favour!" She raised her face and glared at him through wet, furious eyes.

"You should be thanking me for kidnapping you, because you and I both know it was the only way you'd ever really meet a man!"

"What!?"

"I know about all those presentations you've been having. All those poor fellows bowing before you, showing you everything they've got, just trying to get a smile… and you've yet to even consider one of them. You sit there and think, 'Nobody's good enough for the great Princess Nevaeh! Nobody deserves a place with me.' I know if I'd just let you sit there on your throne, you'd have lived alone 'til your death, having never let anyone get close to you. Now I can die a happy man, knowing I'm the only man in history who will ever have his eyes graced with the sight of your bare self!"

She stood open-mouthed through the whole thing, but now that he'd finished…

"Had it never occurred to you why I've yet to choose a husband?" He motioned for her to enlighten him. "In all these presentations I've seen, hour after hour, week after week, the only thing that matters to these men is what they have—what they've done—

that's all they want me to know! Of course I haven't fallen in love! I cannot fall in love with things or actions… I fall in love with people! I have not chosen a husband because none of the suitors have ever let me get to know them. None of them will reveal themselves to me. All they want me to know is what they have and what they've done… nothing about themselves! They won't let me know them! They won't let me love them!"

He stayed still and silent, just watching as she unloaded everything before him.

"They think it dishonourable to simply receive my love without having done something to earn it. So they come with carts full of gold or the head of some poor creature as if to say, 'I've slain this many beasts and that is how much your love is worth,' or, 'I have this much gold and that is how much your love is worth. There. Now I have earned your love, and you will give your love to me because I've bought it.' Now tell me, where is the honour in that?"

She stared at him as if awaiting an answer, but he was too mesmerized to think. After a time, she grabbed the rest of her clothes and marched off into the woods.

"Unlike some of the women you may be familiar with," she said over her shoulder, "my love is not for sale."

DAXION STOOD PROTECTIVELY over Lucas, who sat at his desk in the study sorting through the most recent reports.

"How many?" Lucas asked.

"Almost a thousand."

"Will that be enough?"

"My Lord, I cannot even imagine we will need that many."

"And you can have them all ready and in Hunter's Canyon by morning?"

"That won't be a problem, Sire."

There was a sudden knock at the door, followed by shouting. The door swung open and the guardsman tried to shut it again before the plump maid could run in.

"Let her in," Lucas shouted over the noise. As if the guard could have stopped her anyway, he stepped aside gracefully and shut the door behind the maid, quite out of breath. The maid herself was in a fluster, holding her hands on her hips.

"Why are you here, Gilda?" Lucas asked.

"I let him take her!"

"You were knocked unconscious," said Daxion.

"Too easily. I didn't fight hard enough. I'd do anything to get that poor child back, which is why I'm here to offer my services."

Lucas and Daxion both looked at her in complete confusion.

"Offer your services how?" Lucas inquired.

She gave them both a stern look and shook her finger at them in turn. "Don't play stupid with me. I've seen the kind of folk you're gathering up for this and if anyone is going to sacrifice themselves for that girl, it'll be me!"

The fact that they knew what she was talking about only confused them more.

"Gilda…I am not sure a woman of your stature—"

"And what's wrong with my stature?" She stuck out her chest. Lucas dropped his head into his hands. "You don't know a person's talents from looking at them. I could make good money if I were in that sort of business."

"Nobody is questioning your talents," Daxion said as he walked around the desk and patted her shoulder lovingly. "And your fervour is greatly appreciated, but you can serve us much better here, Gilda."

She looked up at him with stern eyes, as if she felt she weren't being taken seriously. "Well, I'll just present myself to your round-up crew and see what they say. I'm sure they'll know skill when they see it. Permission to leave?"

"Granted," said Lucas with a tired wave of his hand. She opened the door and marched out. Lucas and Daxion looked at each other. "I'll be glad when this is over."

RUTH LAY NEARER to Roy than usual that night as he prodded the fire back at the main camp. He sat on a log, staring intently into the flames. It was still a small fire, not quite ready for cooking, if it ever would be, but his mind was elsewhere.

Nevaeh stepped cautiously out of the pitch-blackness surrounding them and came into the light with her eyes downcast and her scarf wrapped in a bundle. At the sight of Nevaeh coming near the fire, Ruth got up and left. Nevaeh watched her vanish into the forest, then looked at Roy, who gave her a look so blank it said everything. Her eyes lowered again and she unfolded the bundle in her hands.

"Does she like fish?"

Nevaeh revealed three fish the length of her arm and held them out toward Roy. He took them in bewilderment.

"You fish?"

"I know how."

He looked them over for a time before setting them down and admitting, "I don't know how to cook fish."

"Are you going to tie me up again?"

It was then he realized she was still standing.

"It crossed my mind," he said coldly. "I just hope you don't go running off again—unless you've figured out what to do if you're surrounded by wolves." He gestured to the opposite log and she sat down.

"I don't know what got into me," she said apologetically.

"You had some rage to unload. I understand that, and I'm hoping that's all of it."

Since no meat had been cooked, she picked up some of the few fruits they had seen and started eating.

"So what are you looking for?" Roy asked.

She wiped juice from her mouth before saying, "I'm sorry?"

"If you don't want lords and princes with gold and jewellery or dragon-slayers, what is it you want? What does your knight in shining armour look like?"

"Um…" She stopped to think, looking a little flustered. Roy got the impression she already knew the answer and was just grasping for the words. "All I want… all I've wanted from the start was one man who would come to me in these presentations with no gold, no decorations, no titles or beasts or things—just himself. I want him to just bring himself and say, 'You know what, Princess? I don't deserve you. None of these men do. But if you give me the chance, I promise to give you the best of what I am, the best of what I have, the best of what I can do—everyday—if you'll just love me for me.'

"They all feel like they have to prove their worth, prove they're worthy of the throne. None of these men really want me, Roy. They want the kingdom. They want the paradise and the glory. None of them care about the one who provides it. It's the kingdom whose approval they seek, not mine. That's why they come to me, as though I judge things and actions rather than people.

"So many lords enter into royal marriages trying to be something they're not so their wives never get to know them. Or they convince themselves they can never be good enough, so they don't even try, giving their wives absolutely nothing at all. I don't expect my husband to be someone he's not, and I don't want him to give up on himself either. I just want a husband who will give me the best of himself, as much as he is able. Why do all men find that so much to ask?"

Roy stared into the fire he had stopped prodding a long time ago. It was little more than a dim light now. "Because it's not enough."

Nevaeh observed Roy as he struggled with the fire, but her real focus was on herself. What had just happened? What did she just do? She had answered his question without any hesitation whatsoever! When a man asked that kind of question, one didn't just answer! At least, not so directly! Why had she done that?

It may have been the same answer to why she felt safer swimming around him than around her own bodyguards at the palace. Perhaps she felt it was okay to answer because he was so obviously not trying to woo her… or was he? Perhaps this wasn't just a typical kidnapping, as he said. Perhaps this was some bizarre new courting strategy from an eccentric land. No. Somehow that didn't seem like him. He was too straightforward for something that complex… or was he just pretending to be?

The truth was, she knew men who would likely employ such a mind game—Lucas, for one, and maybe half the other men in the palace. She had never felt entirely safe around those men and their all too innocent smiles—especially after she "blossomed." She didn't feel that way around Roy, which made no sense to her whatsoever. Why would she fear men who might possibly consider taking advantage of her, but feel safe when she was in the presence of a man who was so obviously a pervert and made no attempt to hide it?

The answer eluded her. So she observed him with his eyes on the fire. The light had picked up a little, but he still struggled, intently, tenaciously. A warm glow surrounded him and it finally sank in—she did feel safe with him, despite everything he said and did and all common sense. She felt safer and freer here than at the palace.

She extended her hands and feet toward the fire to help keep warm. She observed a glint in Roy's sullen eyes, and from then on his spirits seemed vaguely lifted.

CHAPTER FOUR

The birds were gone again when Nevaeh woke to the warm morning light beaming through the trees. She yawned and stretched and discovered that her hands were again bound to a tree.

A knife launched into the tree startled her to full waking. She sat up as high as she could and saw Roy mounted on Ruth's back.

"It'll take you about three minutes to cut through those ropes. By then I'll be gone." The finality of his words was a stark reminder of why she was here. Once again, his face showed no emotions. "If all goes well, your people will come for you before nightfall. Until then, keep the fire going. That'll keep away most animals. There's enough firewood for a day. When you get hungry, the food's hanging from that branch over there—just untie the rope at the stump to let it down."

He wrapped the reins around his hands.

"So this is goodbye then." She tried to show as little emotion as he did, but she wasn't sure how well she succeeded.

He gave her a curious look. "Yes, it is." They stared at each other for a moment more. "Goodbye, Princess." He turned Ruth around.

"Roy…"

He turned to her again.

She struggled for something to say. What wouldn't sound too mushy, or girly? *Just say anything.* "What do I do if I'm surrounded by wolves?"

It was then she realized that with all his blank stares, all his emotionless faces, he was analyzing her, sizing her up, seeing what she was made of.

After a moment he said, "You pray."

With that, he gave the reins a tug and Ruth unfurled her wings to full span, her wing-studs jingling. With a flap of her massive wings, they took off into the air, disappearing behind the treetops.

LUCAS STOOD SULLENLY in Hunter's Canyon, sweating through his coat. It was another cloudless day and the sunlight had just peered over the cliffs and treetops to beat upon the company in the canyon. The enormous tents provided the only shade, but Lucas had to remain in plain sight—with bodyguards around him, of course. In a vast, bowl-shaped dirt valley surrounded by vine-covered cliffs and forestry, an attack could come from anywhere.

Daxion was speaking with his hired hands, men dressed in disoriented greens and browns, wearing scrambled makeup of the same colours. Bruce had recommended them. He said they were professionals, but no professional dressed like that! Daxion dismissed them and they headed toward the rocky, vine-covered walls. Lucas waved Daxion over.

"All the preparations are made?"

"They are moving into place now, my Lord."

"Then we wait." They both looked around to the cliffs and trees, wondering where the kidnapper might be hiding. "And congratulations on your collection. When he sees what we have brought him, he is bound to return her to us."

"I wouldn't."

Lucas flashed him an intolerant glare, but Daxion appeared oblivious.

"How good are these men you've hired?"

Daxion looked in the direction the men had walked and Lucas' eyes followed. He could see nothing but the canyon walls.

"They are very good."

The heat was so bad that Lucas almost thought he was imagining things when he heard a voice echo "Lord Steward!" across the canyon.

"I am he," Lucas shouted back. Everyone looked around to see where the voice was coming from. Daxion pointed a wavering finger to a cliff wall straight ahead. "Where is Nevaeh?"

"She is safe," the voice answered. "Did you bring what I requested?"

"Indeed… can you see?"

"I see everything."

Lucas looked around again. "In that case, feast your eyes on these." He turned to the tent keeper. "Bring them out!"

Out of the tent stepped a young woman dressed in silks and jewellery. She walked at a slow, steady pace from the tent. Then another young woman came out after her, followed by another, and another. The women all proceeded to walk slowly in a large circle, several strides apart. They all wore exotic clothes, makeup, and jewellery.

"You requested that I bring you women," Lucas called to the cliff wall. "Women beautiful enough to trade the Princess for. Here you are! Women found from all across the land. All of them young and beautiful. Many of them are virgins. Others are experienced mistresses. Some can even dance!" He motioned to the tent keeper and clusters of women were brought out to dance in the circle the other women walked around. "Pick any you like, and as many as you like—as many as you think you can handle! Surrender Nevaeh and you can have anything your heart desires."

Roy sat huddled in a tiny crevice in the cliff wall, the only path to which was a cave that led all the way back to the forest. Wrapped in a grey cloak, Roy could see everyone up close through his telescope. He was truly disappointed. The women were attractive enough, most of them, but he was after something more. These women were all the same. He could tell by their eyes, their faces, the way they walked... he'd been involved with women like that before. He may have even been with these exact women before.

Was that it? Were all women really the same? *Not Nevaeh. She's... No, I won't go there. I need a woman like me—as bad as me. I won't drag her into... Don't make it about her feelings! It's not about what's good for her... it's about what I need! I don't need her! I need...*

He peered through the telescope to watch the dancers. They were quite good. Was that what he needed? He used to think so, but he had lived that life for so long.

Well, what did you expect? Did you actually think asking for a parade of women would provide something different from what you've been seeing all your life? All these women are the same! The only woman that's ever been different...

He dropped the telescope. He had stopped paying attention a long time ago. He promised himself he wouldn't do this, promised himself it wouldn't happen. She was just supposed to be another woman, just another means to what he really wanted. Why did she have to...?

LUCAS STOOD IN confusion. Despite asking the voice a couple of times whether or not he was enjoying the show, he had not heard a word from the cliff wall since the display began. Had Daxion's men found him?

"Enough!" The voice startled Lucas witless. "End the display!"

That was all. The voice went silent. Lucas gathered his wits back. "Have you made a decision? Whom do you desire?"

Dead silence. Even the dancers stood still as everyone awaited a response.

"Come back tomorrow. You will have my decision then."

Tomorrow? After all this!

"Show us the Princess!" Lucas demanded.

"Come back tomorrow!"

That final command was loud enough to scare half of the people gathered in the valley. The women cautiously walked back to the tents, looking uncertainly at Lucas for permission. Lucas and Daxion gave each other perplexed and irritated looks.

Nevaeh sprinkled some seasoning on the rabbits as she turned them on the spit over the fire. She tried to remember how much seasoning Roy had used before. How long had it been since she cooked her own meal? She wasn't sure what it was, but there was something rejuvenating about cooking. She might even try cooking the fish she caught for Ruth.

She froze when the birds stopped singing. Looking up, she saw Ruth fly in over the treetops and land some distance from the fire. Roy's face was again expression-less, but it seemed forced this time, and he deliberately avoided looking at her.

"How did it go?" she asked cautiously.

"I don't know," he said quietly as he jumped off Ruth and marched back into the forest.

"Well, is someone coming for—?"

"I don't know!"

And he was gone again. Ruth followed after him, giving Nevaeh a short, curious glance. Nevaeh was alone again, and deeply worried.

CHIPS OF WOOD flew off the tree as Roy beat it savagely with his axe. The wedge had been growing, but now it was accompanied by several little nicks scattered ran-domly around it. Finally dropping his axe, he pushed on the tree with all his might but it wouldn't budge. He threw his weight into it, punched and yelled at it, but still nothing. Giving up, he stood back and roared at it. Ruth walked over, gave it a headbutt, and the tree toppled with a loud crash.

Roy stood over the stump, struggling to catch his breath. Once he could speak again, he turned to Ruth.

"When I want your help, I'll ask for it!"

Stricken, Ruth turned around and walked away with her head lowered.

"Come 'ere," Roy said as he rubbed his head, "Come 'ere!" He pointed to the ground right in front of him and Ruth obeyed with her eyes down. He stroked the front of her face. "I'm sorry. I'm not mad at you. Alright?" She purred deeply as he scratched behind her ears. "Come on, let's find some supper."

IT WAS NIGHT by the time Nevaeh saw Roy return to the camp, dragging a deer behind him. She was standing over the fire once again, turning rodents on a spit. Roy paused at the sight of her standing over the fire. Ruth dropped the bodies she carried in her mouth and walked back into the forest.

"You're cooking?" asked Roy in a much more sombre tone than when he left.

"I didn't know when you'd be back." She hid her anger well despite being worried sick for the past few hours over what was going to happen to her.

"Sorry." He grabbed a piece of meat she'd already cooked and bit into it.

Nevaeh froze and stared at him, frowning. He was apologizing now? What had happened? "I was trying to do it like you. Did I use too much seasoning?"

"No, this is good." He went back to the dead deer, grabbed a long rope, and threw it over a high branch.

"I cooked some fish, too, for Ruth to try." She walked over to the large stone where lay the prepared fish and the knife she had used to clean them, the same knife he had given her to cut herself free. She picked it up and stared at it, gripping it tightly, taking in the feel of it. She watched how the firelight danced awkwardly on its edges; it had collected a lot of stains in its time with Roy. She looked back to her kidnapper. His back was turned to her, pulling on the rope to raise the dead buck off the ground to hang by its hind legs. He was totally focused on his work.

She walked over to him quietly, held the knife by the blade, extended the handle toward him, and said, "Do you need this?"

He turned around, saw the knife in her hands, and said, "Yes, thank you." He took it and began stripping the deer.

Nevaeh sat down on the nearest log and watched Roy at work. She didn't watch the work itself, which was rather unpleasant, but there was something about the vigour, the sense of duty with which Roy worked that she found strangely fascinating.

But she could not focus on that for long. Now that he seemed to have calmed down, it was time she had her answer.

"Roy, what happened today?"

He paused, and then with an effort went back to his work. "I couldn't go through with it."

She watched his face carefully. The stone, emotionless wall was gradually and reluctantly falling apart, but what lay on the other side was such a jumble of mixed emotions that it was no easier to interpret.

"Why not?"

He stared into blank space for a long time before answering. "I guess I figured that whatever they offer me in return, you'll always be worth more."

At that, Nevaeh didn't know what to think. She fell silent for a time, trying to gather her own thoughts before coming back with, "So… what now?"

Roy stopped completely with a great, frustrated sigh. He leaned against the meat and rested his head on his arms.

"I don't know," he answered. Then he looked at her with those studious eyes, intent as if everything of importance rested on him accurately analyzing her very next move. "What do you want to happen?"

She almost missed how vulnerable those eyes had become, analytical as they were as they stared at her, demanding an answer.

Overwhelmed, she lowered her eyes and answered, "I don't know, either."

When she looked up again, he nodded with understanding, then took down the meat and placed it over the fire. Now she was worried, for he was no longer looking at her.

"Perhaps we can decide together over some drinks." He looked at her again, with another inquisitive look. "You Royals do drink, don't you?"

She gave him a friendly smile. "On occasion."

His own lips curved a little. He cleaned off his hands, grabbed a lighted stick, and walked away.

"Keep rotating the deer," he said as he headed toward the forest. "When there's no more red, that means it's ready."

She jumped to her feet, but he was gone before she

could protest, so she turned the spit as she had seen him do before. When her arms got tired, she let it rest for a time and sat back down, trying to calm herself. What was she doing? The man was fetching drinks, and she was cooking dinner! When she realized she was combing her hair with her fingers, she forced her hands down to her lap, then straightened the frock she was wearing. Why would she bother with such a thing? She didn't like anything she had on anyway. This was all his kinky rubbish! She stopped herself again when she realized she was adjusting the corset, then jumped back to her feet and rotated the deer despite her arms still aching.

Roy came back carrying a bottle of rum and two wine glasses. His hands were jittering nervously.

"Do you have any water left?" she said quickly.

He looked up at her startled, then answered, "Oh, sure."

He set the glasses down and grabbed the flask at his side to pour water into her glass. He then poured some rum for himself.

He sat down on the log and gave her the water. It wasn't until she took it and said, "Thank you," that he looked her in the eyes again and smiled.

She sat down next to him and silently tried to still her breathing while he threw back a big swig of his drink. She took a long, slow sip from her glass. The cool clean water soothed her throat as it went down, bringing a brief chill to her chest.

"How is it?" he asked quietly.

"It's perfect," she said with a nervous smile.

He smiled gladly, then blinked.

"Oh, I gotta feed Ruth. I'll be right back." He stood up.

"Wait, give her the fish."

Roy spotted the fish on the rock and picked them up. He looked at Nevaeh and grinned. "She'll like this."

He took the fish and cooked deer and walked into the darker woods. Nevaeh could hear Ruth's earrings jingle as her master approached; she thought it was cute, and had another sip. Roy returned and sat back down beside Nevaeh.

"She could smell you on them," he said.

"Is that good?"

"Oh yeah. She really likes you."

They both stared into the fire. He had another swig of rum, and she had a gulp of water.

"So tell me about yourself," he said.

Nevaeh looked at him, confused. "You already know about me."

"I want to know more," he said adamantly. "I want to know everything."

"You mean my life story?"

"Yeah."

She turned her face to the fire, open-mouthed. "Well… there's not much to tell. I was born a princess… I've been a princess all my life. I have a lot of servants and a big room with a view. Life's been good to me." She turned back to him and those studious eyes. "That's it. How about you?"

His attention went to the fire. He spoke slowly at first, maintaining an emotionless face. "I was born in the Minland prairies. My mother was a Stonewalker, my father was a Stonewalker… and they raised me accordingly. My father had a job in town. I don't really know what he did—I didn't see him much. When he was home, he'd always work the fields alone. So I spent most of my time with my mother. She taught me how to be a Stonewalker, to know right from wrong. And whenever I messed up, she'd forgive me—give me some light discipline and forgive me. She was very strict, but she was also very loving. So when I met Annie and married her, I assumed that all women would be as forgiving as my mother." He took a big swig of rum and gulped it down.

"I was wrong. Once I married Annie, there was no room for forgiveness, no room for mistakes. We were to be a family of Stonewalkers with no ill marks. This was especially true when I took a job as an Ambassador of the Stone. I took the job because it paid well and I needed to provide for whatever Annie decided she needed. But I knew it wouldn't suit me. One had to keep up certain appearances. One had to wear a certain smile, say certain things, hold his wife a certain way. Any sign of discontent over anything would be seen as a lack of faith or the result of some secret, evil deed.

"I was fired from my job while Annie was seven

months into her first pregnancy. So I asked them for another job and they gave me one in utilities—something in the background. But it didn't pay well and Annie was never satisfied with that.

"I suppose it was shortly after Brian was born that I started spending my time at the taverns. I got more affection from my fellow drinkers than I did at home. And there were times when the women in those places seemed more beautiful than her. Of course they weren't—it was just the makeup, but… the first time a woman offered herself to me for a fair price…

"I don't know how much Annie knew. I feel like she had that suspicious glare ever since we were first married. As Brian grew up, she didn't let me spend much time with him, afraid my evil ways might seep into him somehow. That didn't bother me much, though. I knew it was probably true, and I had nothing to offer him— no words of advice, no life skills. And he had adopted his mother's eyes."

His eyes glistened, as if the light reflected off tears frozen permanently inside him.

"It was after the death of our second child that I left her, looking for my place in the world. I knew I didn't belong with a family of Stonewalkers. If perfection was possible, it wouldn't be achieved with me. I joined a band of pirates sailing along the West Coast. It was only with them that I didn't feel less than human. I finally found a lifestyle where I didn't have to be good, didn't have to care. I had all the money, power, and women I could want. But something was still missing.

"I still didn't feel at home. I was in one of the most vile groups in the world and I didn't belong, because as much as I tried not to care who I hurt, not to care about what I did or the consequences, I couldn't deny that this wasn't who I was. I realized that whenever I messed up, it wasn't because I didn't care. I did care. I wanted to do good. I just couldn't live up to anyone's standards of good.

"When I became powerful enough to work on my own, I went out in search of true happiness. I looked everywhere for female companions, but anyone I had a relationship with was just like Annie—oh, they had different standards of perfection, even opposite ones at times, but the fact remained that if I didn't live up to their standards in everything I did, I had no place with them.

"Hired women are no better for me, because even though they demand nothing… that's just it—they demand nothing. They're trained to sit still and keep their mouths shut unless you say otherwise. They have no opinions, no objections, no feeling, no love. They challenge nothing, they arouse nothing. There is nothing in them that calls me to be anybody, and so I become nobody—not even myself.

He paused again. She wasn't sure if he was even breathing.

"So many times I've thought about just going back to Minland, going back to Annie, trying to raise Brian however I can. But I know that won't work. Seeing me again will just bring her more pain. Everything in me wants to make things right, and nothing in me knows how. Constantly I pray that Brian will think me dead. That's all I'm good for now. I know what it's like to have a father who is around but not there. That's the only thing I can give my son now, the only thing I have to offer him is permission to cry—the right to cry, and to move on without me."

Nevaeh did not know how long she sat there paralyzed, just staring unblinking at the man beside her. The numbness of his voice, that he could speak those words with such dead emotion, was almost eerie. She blinked for the first time in an eternity and looked into the fire, allowing it all to sink in.

After a moment of watching the fire, she had another sip of water and then nodded decisively. "Okay."

Roy gave her a puzzled look. "Okay?"

"Okay." She met his eyes. "My life story. My best memories are of my father. I've always been high maintenance, but that's never bothered him. He treated me more like a princess than anyone else did. When I was young, he used to take me for trips into the woods, just the two of us. He taught me how to fish and how to cook. Even though we had servants at the palace who cooked and cleaned for us all the time, he taught me how to look after myself. Work is important to him, but it isn't about getting something done—for him it's just the work itself, the act of doing it, even if the results aren't great. The first time we baked together, the cake wasn't very good because he let me choose the ingredients. But it didn't matter to him. He just wanted to make a cake with me.

"I never knew my mother, but I've had many substitutes—mostly in the maids. I used to see my Aunt Mary once or twice a year, but she lives far off in the north, and her visits became less frequent after Lucas took the throne. She always used to bring me pretty dresses from the Northlands. But the last few times she's visited, she seemed so sad…

"When my father left to seek land in the West—that was when I really got attached to Gilda. For the longest time, people looked at me as though I had lost something I would never get back. Everyone saw me as a walking tragedy—but not Gilda. She never saw me as hopeless.

"A lot of people felt abandoned when my father left. Some said he left because he was tired of the bickering, all the complaints the people threw at him daily. But they're wrong. My father wouldn't abandon them—not forever. He's a prophet. He said he would return, on a red sunrise, and I believe him. Of course, when they elected Lucas to take over, things got worse—the rioting, for one.

"Sometimes I would put on commoners' clothes and sneak out of the palace by the secret doorway I found in my room, and just walk among the people—feel the crowd, smell their breath—just to see what it's like to live as a commoner.

"Rioters swarm my carriage every other time we go somewhere and I hear people shout to me, 'You Royals, you don't know what it's like! You don't know the suffering we endure! You don't know how hard it is in these times!' But I do know… and it breaks my heart that they elected Lucas to rule them. They shouldn't have elected anyone in the first place, but since it's done, I wish they'd elect Daxion to replace him. He's not perfect by any means, but I know his heart, and if there's one good man with the charisma to replace Lucas, it's Daxion." She sighed regretfully. "But I know he would never agree to that, not with his loyalties being what they are. I'm not worried, though, because my father will reclaim the throne one day and restore prosperity to the kingdom."

She glanced at Roy to gauge his reaction. He seemed to be listening intently, staring once again with those studious eyes that seemed to be growing more personal. "So the best days I've had so far are those spent with my father. And that's why I know that the best days are ahead of me." She gave him a shy smile. "And that's me."

What it was she saw in his eyes now, she couldn't say, but they had grown much more intent and intimate. Before she knew it, he was leaning towards her and gave her a kiss. It was a cautious kiss, and awkward, as if he were accustomed to something more coarse but trying to tone it down into something proper. He seemed uncertain if he was doing it right, all the while wanting to do more. It was tame and unrhythmic and his stubble scratched her, but all those flaws were at the back of her mind as she opened her lips to receive his.

He pulled back and studied her further with the same intimate gaze. She bit her lips as if taking in the aftertaste.

"Does that decrease my value?" she asked.

He grinned and shook his head softly. "Not at all."

They peered into each other's eyes for a moment. Then she leaned forward and gave him the most princess-like kiss she could muster. She hadn't had much practice, but she thought if she brushed his lips gently and then kissed with slow, elegant rhythm, that might be good enough.

Even so, she was nervous and maybe pulled back a bit earlier than she should have. She tried to give him an alluring look, despite the shyness starting to overcome her. The look he gave her in return was so strong it was almost scary. The intent in his eyes had fully ignited. He threw himself upon her and all she managed was a squeak before the two of them toppled over the log and onto the ground. All the passion he'd been holding inside rushed out in a raging torrent. Overwhelmed for the moment, she lay helpless in his arms—until her strength came back and she forced herself on top of him. Suddenly her wits returned and she pulled herself away.

"Wait."

To her astonishment, he relented immediately, fell on his back, and exhaled deeply.

On her knees, recovering her own breath, Nevaeh reached into her sleeve, pulled out the necklace her father had given her, and presented it to Roy. Roy rose to his knees with a curious glance. Nevaeh looked him straight in the eyes to convey the weight of what she was about to do. He seemed bewildered and humbled.

"This is the necklace my father gave me before he left on his expedition. He told me that one day I would meet a man whom I would favour, and I would give this necklace to him. He and I would then be instantly bound to each other. I would be his and he would be mine—forever." She leaned forward an inch. "Do you understand?"

Roy grew a worried frown. "Are you sure about this?"

She nodded resolutely. "Yes."

He looked at the necklace and then back at her. "Isn't it a bit soon?"

She blinked, but her gaze lost none of its gravity. "Our relationship cannot go any further until this is done."

Roy let his head drop. "Okay," he said submissively.

Nevaeh leaned forward with the necklace ready.

"Wait!" Roy urged. She stopped. Roy raised his head to look her in the eyes once again. "Why me?"

Shocked that he didn't already know the answer, she held the sincerity in her voice and told him, "Because you're the only man I've ever met who has recognized his condition and wants to change. You're the only one who has ever been honest with me. You're the only one I trust. You're the only one whom I feel can accept my love as a gift without having to earn it. Will you not let me love you?"

Roy lowered his head again, struggle in his eyes. His eyes moved back and forth as though he was telling himself all the reasons not to do this, all the reasons why he wasn't good enough. Beyond all the struggle in his eyes, a look of sheer gratitude broke through. He shut his eyes hard and failed to suppress a single tear that hurried down his cheek and retreated under his chin.

With gleaming eyes, he looked to her again, now as resolute as she was, and said with bowed head, "I will."

With a final nod, Nevaeh reached her hands around his neck and sealed the clasps. Her hands went warmly to his shoulders, and then back to her lap. He held the pendant in his hands wondrously, still taking in the significance.

She waited until he looked at her again, eyes astonished that she was there, humbled and thankful that she was there, and his eyes began to take in the beauty of her form once again. She moved forward, held his head in her hands, and kissed him softly. He wrapped his arms around her and they fell together onto the grass.

CHAPTER FIVE

A pestering sparrow roused Roy from a good dream. It was still morning when he woke, covered in nothing but a thin shirt, long johns, and the leopard blanket. A cloudy sky dimmed the sunlight and a cool breeze blew through the forest, gently rustling the trees. He looked to the side of him and there lay Nevaeh, fast asleep, relaxed, her chest rising and falling calmly. He rose carefully so he wouldn't disturb her, grabbed a cloak, put on his boots, and went for a walk.

He felt autumn in the air as he paced through the forest. He had not walked far but had already seen rabbit, fox, and deer tracks, all relatively fresh. They would have their choice of breakfast this morning.

"Ruth!" Roy called. It wasn't like her to sleep so far from camp. And it wasn't like her not to answer on the first call, either. He stood still. "Ruth!"

Throwing his cloak aside, he launched himself

back in the direction of the camp, trampling all the twigs in his path with loud cracks, disregarding how much sound was made. He raced past trees and leaped over logs in single strides, not falling once. Never had such primal fear gripped him as he felt now. His heart beat so fast it should have shattered his ribs.

He leaped back into the campsite. Nevaeh was nowhere to be found. He froze in disbelief as a dozen men painted in green and brown appeared from out of nowhere, each one aiming a nocked arrow at his chest. He raised his hands slowly and tried to slow his breathing. He heard a noise and turned around. There was Nevaeh in her nightgown being held by two men. One of them had his hand over her mouth. She had the most horrible look of pain and regret in her eyes. Then stepped out a man all in robes, Lord Lucas, a murderous smile on his face.

"Been having your way with her, I see?" Lucas said. "Bind him."

NEVAEH SCREAMED AT the top of her lungs, fighting with the two men holding her by the arms. It wasn't until Lucas said, almost inaudibly, "Let her go," that the men finally did. With the sudden release, she accidentally threw herself onto the ground, then looked up at Lucas with pure hatred.

She quickly rose to her feet and shouted at him. "How dare you have me manhandled and silenced!"

"You were trying to warn your kidnapper of the

trap! My Lady, what has gotten into you!"

"What will you do to him?"

"He has kidnapped the Princess. He will be punished accordingly once we return. By tomorrow's sunrise, he will be executed."

She ran up to him and shouted in his face, "He has done nothing to harm me since the night he took me!"

Lucas flinched with his hand over his nose and stared at her as though she were some stray, disease-ridden animal. He grabbed her hand and sniffed her arm, made a sound of disgust, then threw it aside like a soiled sheet. "My Lady, you need seeing to." Then he said to the guards, "Get the Princess into a carriage and take her back to the palace."

The two strange men grabbed her again and carried her with her feet kicking and her throat screeching.

DAXION PACED NERVOUSLY outside the Princess' chambers. He had not been permitted to follow the hunters after they returned to camp with word that they had located the Princess. Instead he was ordered to return to the palace and await their arrival. But the waiting had been difficult. Word had just spread through the palace that Lucas had returned and was escorting the Princess to her chambers. So here Daxion waited to be sure she was alright.

The sound of large doors bursting open echoed through the hall, followed immediately by shrill screams. Lucas was indeed escorting Nevaeh to her chambers, his hand firmly gripping her arm. She fought with him all the way. A few guards followed close by.

With one strong jerk, she forced her arm free, clasped the wall, and broke into sobs, her body a heap of spasms. Lucas flashed patronizing smiles to any servants who passed by and glared at the Princess with hands on his hips. When he tried to grab her arm again, she swatted it aside and continued to cry into the wall.

After a time she carried herself, on her own feet, to her chamber door, sliding against the wall. The guard standing there opened it a touch and she disappeared through the slit. The guard shut the door behind her and cut off the sound of her moping. The guards that followed Lucas took their own positions around the door. Daxion's eyes shifted to Lucas. He realized then that Lucas had been eyeing him for a long time with those accusing, all too knowing eyes.

"Don't let her out until she's calmed down," Lucas said to the guards before stepping toward Daxion.

"What has happened?" Daxion asked when Lucas stopped in front of him.

"She is hysterical," Lucas said almost before Daxion finished. "It has been a trying ordeal for her, as I am sure you are aware. She is delirious. She is just far too happy to be back!" He stopped to wipe some spittle off his chin.

"Perhaps someone should—"

"I have no doubt what sort of duty you would wish to fulfill, Lord Captain, but that position is already being filled as you see." He gestured briefly toward the guards. "You know your business."

Daxion nodded with no enthusiasm. "I do."

"Then be about it."

Daxion stood, feet planted, and stared Lucas in the eyes—those hateful, angry eyes. Yet… they were the eyes of the kingdom. He bowed in compliance.

"As my Lord wishes."

He caught a glimpse of a spiteful, satisfied grin on Lucas' face before walking away, to his duties.

ROY WAS ON his knees in a cell with no light, his hands held up by chains hanging from opposite sides of the room. The sting of the initial beating was slowly wearing off, leaving in its place a throbbing pain. He ached in many places, mostly his face. He felt around the inside of his teeth with his tongue and noticed more than one empty space. He may have swallowed one. How much of his own blood had he swallowed? Fortunately they hadn't stripped him yet or they may have noticed the necklace—what would that have cost him?

There was an ear-piercing screech of metal, and then the door came open. Men with torches entered, followed by an expressionless man with a satchel. Roy thought he heard the guard outside address the man as "Lord Captain." Now that there was light again, Roy could see from his unswollen eye that there was a chair and table in the room.

The two guards with torches stood on either side of him and the captain took the chair in front of him, opened the satchel, and poured sharp, metal shards onto the table. Putting the satchel aside, the captain took a leather whip and began picking pieces of metal off the table and attaching them to the whip, his eyes low the whole time, focused on his work.

The guards grabbed the back of Roy's shirt and tore it open. He panicked for a second before getting his breathing back under control. The man in front of him kept his eyes low, equipping the whip shard by shard.

So that was it—they weren't even going to bother with questions. Not even look him in the eye. They had already made their decision.

"I never hurt her."

He didn't expect that to stop it; he just wanted it to be known.

The man finally looked him in the eyes. He had bright, piercing blue eyes. But there was something odd in the way he looked at Roy, as if he knew something. In the man's eyes Roy was surprised to find, deep down, a look of respect, and of sorrow. But deeper than that it was, ultimately, a look of impotence.

"I believe you."

The man's stare lingered just long enough to be certain that Roy understood. Then, having prepared the whip, he got up off the chair and circled around behind Roy. Roy took in a deep breath and tried his best to brace himself—to take it like a man without screaming or crying—a plan that lasted until the first crack tore a slit in his back.

As soon as Gilda entered the Princess' chambers and saw her lying, sulking on her bed, she ran toward her with quiet words of comfort. Nevaeh sat up and held her arms out to Gilda as soon as she heard her voice, and Gilda embraced her, sitting up on the bed and rocking her in her arms.

"Shhh… Child, it's alright. I'm here. You're safe now. Shhh…"

How long she sat, just holding her and whispering to her, she didn't know, and she didn't care. Gilda was overwhelmed with relief at seeing her alive, and overcome with grief at seeing her in this state. She just sat there rocking and let the time go by.

Eventually Nevaeh lifted her wet face and spoke in words almost indiscernable through her cries and heavy breathing. "He never did anything to hurt me. He was good to me. He fed me and clothed me. He's not a bad person."

"That kidnapper, you mean?"

Nevaeh nodded with her head low.

Gilda sighed. "You're quite taken with him, aren't you?" She nodded again. "Is there anything I can do to ease this for you, dear?"

Nevaeh paused for a moment and then looked back up at Gilda with new life in her glistening, wet eyes.

"Have you finished my ball gown?"

The metal shrieking caught Roy's attention as the cell door opened again. In stepped Nevaeh in a gown with one of the largest bottoms he had ever seen. At the sight of him, she wore an understandably horrified look. She hung the torch on the wall, and as soon as the guard shut the door behind her she bent down to kiss him. He flinched back at first from the sting of his busted lip, but then ignored it, and just let her mouth embrace his. When she pulled back, she had a speck of blood on her lips.

"I can get you out of here," she said frantically.

He exhaled and said in a dead voice, "Why?"

She gave him a hurt glare. "What?"

"Why bother getting me out?"

Now she looked insulted. "Because I love you."

"Why me?"

"You know why! Because you're the only man I've ever met who feels real!"

"You'll find another! There's got to be someone else out there who's less trouble than me!"

She glared at him with stern eyes, then drew her attention to his chest, reached into his shirt, pulled out the necklace, and held it tight in front of his face. "Do you know what this means?"

"Yes."

"No, you don't! If you really knew what it meant you wouldn't tell me to just forget about you! This around your neck means we are one! This means I own you! This means I won't let you give up!"

"Princess… even if you broke me out of here, I can't follow you anywhere. I don't even have the strength to stand up, let alone walk."

"And yet you won't ask me to carry you!"

Roy lowered his head.

"All I'm asking is that you try," Naveah said. "That you give me whatever strength you have, and let me take care of the rest. Will you deny me even that? Roy… will you answer my call or not?"

The Princess left the cell wearing a downcast, defeated look. The guard observed her as she walked away, slowly, with one hand on the wall and the other on her forehead.

She walked like that all the way back to her bedroom chamber, graciously refusing any help the servants offered her. When she entered her bedroom and the door shut behind her, she ran straight to her dresser, uncovering Roy who had crawled under her the whole way.

"We can get to the streets from here by my secret passage," she said in a hurry. "We'll need to wear peasants' clothes. I've got some in my costume drawer."

She went to her bed and dumped all the ragged clothes on top of it. She then removed her gown to put the street clothes on and froze when she saw the streaks of blood on the crinoline. She looked to Roy's slashed back and noticed he was lying facedown on the floor.

"You need to get up," she urged with her hand on his arm. "We don't have much time."

LUCAS SAT ON his throne with Theodius sitting on a decorated chair to his right and Daxion standing by his left. He was listening to another one of Theodius' plans on taxing bridge passes when two guards ran into the throne room.

"My Lord!" one shouted. "We went into the kidnapper's cell to serve him his last meal and he is gone!"

"It was the Princess who freed him!" said the other. "At least, that's what the keeper told us!"

Theodius nearly burst out of his seat. "Well, don't just stand there! Find—!"

Lucas grabbed Theodius' arm to halt him, and then said in a calm tone, "If she attempts to free a prisoner I have condemned to death… does that disqualify her for the throne?"

Theodius sat back and thought to himself. "I don't know, my Lord. I would have to check the scrolls and the ancient—"

"Then to be safe…" He stood up, gave the guards a commanding glare, and said, "Find them!"

IT WAS EARLY morning. The sun had not yet risen, but already the clouds in the sky lit up with shades of red, pink, and purple. The cobblestone streets were still quiet as most commoners and salesmen would not awake for another hour. A cool breeze blew and whispered through the alleys.

In a ragged cloak and hood, Nevaeh led the way holding Roy's hand, trying to hurry though aware of his exhaustion. She had to get him to safety before he finally wore out, and before anyone noticed the blood already soaking through his coat.

Down by the docks, she found a sailboat with a man loosing the ropes. It was ready for taking off. She walked onto the dock and pulled out some gold pieces with her free hand. Roy was bent half over from wheezing.

"Excuse me, sir," she said. "May I please have this boat? I will pay you enough to buy another one."

The man looked her over and stepped out onto the deck, grinning. "You're a pretty little thing," he said. "Maybe I want something else."

The next thing she knew, Roy's fist appeared where the man's face had been, and he fell into the water with a great splash. Roy then fell onto the boards, completely out of breath.

"No, you don't!" she yelled at him as she heaved him up. "Come on! We're almost safe!"

She managed to pick him up and drop him onto the boat, toppling in like luggage. Then Nevaeh jumped in, cut the ropes, made sure the sail was at full mast, and even grabbed two paddles. But she didn't need the paddles—the wind was already carrying the sailboat away from the docks, away from the land. She put down the paddles and ran over to Roy to be sure he was still conscious.

"Where are we going, Nevaeh?" he asked, his voice full of exhaustion.

"The land isn't safe right now. I doubt we can even

sail along the coast. We'll head west."

"There's nothing in the West!"

"Then it's the last place they'll think to look for us! Just lie back and relax, but don't die on me!"

As they moved out to sea, she aimed the boat toward a single cloud at the horizon where a clear dividing line marked the border between blue earth and orange sky. The wind picked up and the sky grew increasingly red.

LUCAS, THEODIUS, AND Daxion searched through the streets along with every available guard. A few commoners had already stepped out into the streets and were pushed aside or held against walls until the guards were satisfied that they were who they said they were. Lucas watched the escalating chaos with frustration until one guard returned from the docks and shouted for everyone to follow him.

Once they reached the docks, Lucas took out his telescope and looked to the speck where the guard pointed. Sure enough, there were those two idiots heading for the red horizon.

"What do they think they are doing? Riding on a little sailboat…" He put down the telescope and turned to Daxion. "Where is your ship?"

THE WIND HAD died down and Nevaeh resorted to the paddles. Roy lay inside the boat watching the shore move further and further away until the castle of Al-landor was the only piece of land he still recognized. The only objects getting bigger were the four or five ships heading in their direction, like silver beasts on the prowl.

"What now?" Roy asked.

Nevaeh wore a grave look. "Now we pray."

LUCAS STOOD AT the very front of the *Sea Phoenix*, Daxion's ship, watching his prey draw closer and closer despite their vain efforts to escape. The still sea beneath him seemed severed in two by the great hull as water spurted out of the incision and filled the air with va-pour. Daxion stepped up beside him on deck.

"Every other fast ship is in this pursuit, my Lord. One of us is bound to catch them." There was an un-common lack of enthusiasm in Daxion's tone, but Lu-cas ignored it.

"It won't be long now," Lucas said. A sudden gust struck the ship. It tilted slightly to the side and creaked, then gradually returned to level. The sea before him began to churn in tiny waves. Lucas grinned. "This es-cape was doomed from the start."

FEELING THE WIND pick up again, Nevaeh set the sail, and it was immediately torn apart by a savage gust. The mast split in two and fell over. They almost lost the paddles as the boat tilted in the waves. The horizon before them had suddenly turned blurry and grey, unlike the rest of the sky above them. The wind blew harder, rousing the waves, rocking the boat from side to side. The air around her filled with vapour that blew into her face and drenched her clothes.

Roy crawled toward her with the paddles and grabbed tightly onto her hand.

LUCAS COULD HARDLY believe what he was seeing. The once clear horizon suddenly a haze, the border between earth and sky suddenly vanished. He could hardly keep track of the sailboat as the escalating waves tossed it about. The waves began to take their toll on the passengers of the *Sea Phoenix* as well. The violent rocking back and forth was enough to turn any man's stomach.

Then out of the horizon came a most terrifying sight.

THE WAVES RAGING toward Roy and Nevaeh had begun to tower. Massive bodies of water smacked into the boat, clearing away the paddles and splintering the structure. Roy and Nevaeh held on to each other tightly, the world around them ever turning, spiralling as their vessel broke apart and they lost all sense of direction and gravity itself.

And on came the wall.

LUCAS STOOD PETRIFIED at the beast that emerged from out of the mist, a "fifty-footer" he heard someone shout. How water could stand on itself that long without crashing was a pure mystery. The monster wave swallowed up the tiny sailboat from their sight, like a fly in the mouth of a great lion. The boat disappeared, buried under the clap of the wave. Then no more waves arose.

Suddenly the wind died down, the sea fell eerily silent, and the mist lifted. The horizon returned, blue earth and red sky separated once again. The sea sparkled with clear, brilliant light, and the clouds drifted apart.

Lucas stared at the spot where the boat should have been, where it should have risen by now if there was any part of it still able to float, but even through his telescope he found nothing.

"Where'd they go?" he yelled in frustration. "What happened? Where are they?"

Daxion, standing by his side, looked out toward the horizon with an unfamiliar calm and peace in his eyes. "They've gone to the land beyond the sea."

Lucas planted his fists on the rail, his eyes low, and exhaled all his frustration. After a time, he walked back to the man at the rudder and told him to head back.

But Daxion lingered a little longer at the front, his eyes on the horizon, waiting for the sunrise.